# RAINBOW RHINO

*story and pictures by*

# PETER SIS

ALFRED A. KNOPF · NEW YORK

*This is a Borzoi Book published by Alfred A. Knopf, Inc.*

Copyright © 1987 by Peter Sis.
All rights reserved under International and Pan-American Copyright Conventions.
Published in the United States by Alfred A. Knopf, Inc., New York,
and simultaneously in Canada by Random House of Canada Limited, Toronto.
Distributed by Random House, Inc., New York.
Manufactured in Singapore
1   3   5   7   9   10   8   6   4   2

Library of Congress Cataloging-in-Publication Data

Sis, Peter. Rainbow Rhino.

Summary: Rhino's good friends, the rainbow birds, leave him for better places
to live, but they soon discover that beautiful places can have secret dangers.
[1. Rhinoceros—Fiction.   2. Birds—Fiction] I. Title.
PZ7.S6219Rai   1987   [E]   87-2679
ISBN 0-394-89009-4   ISBN 0-394-99009-9 (lib. bdg.)

*For Frances and Kate*

Somewhere behind the mountains
in the middle of a deep valley
lived the Rainbow Rhinoceros.

Rhino was happy with life as it was.
He had plenty of space to run in,
the sun to warm him,
the breeze to cool him,
and his good friends, the rainbow birds.

They played hide-and-seek with him.
They told one another stories,
and they took long walks together.

One day they walked farther than they
had ever been before.
They left the valley
and started up the mountain.

"What a strange and wonderful place," thought Rhino
as they pushed their way through the wild forest
and came to a blue lake.

"What a beautiful lake!" said the blue bird.
He flew from Rhino's back and gazed at the clear water.
"I want to stay here," he said.
So his friends went on without him.

Soon they came to a grove of ripe bananas.
"What a lovely sight!" said the yellow bird.
He fluttered from Rhino's back to get a closer look.
"I want to stay here," he said.
So Rhino and the red bird left him there.

They wandered out of the forest
and into a field of bright poppies.
"How wonderful!" said the red bird
as he jumped from poppy to poppy.
"I want to stay here," he said.
And Rhino was left alone.

He walked sadly on, dragging his feet,
until he came to a bare and lonely tree.

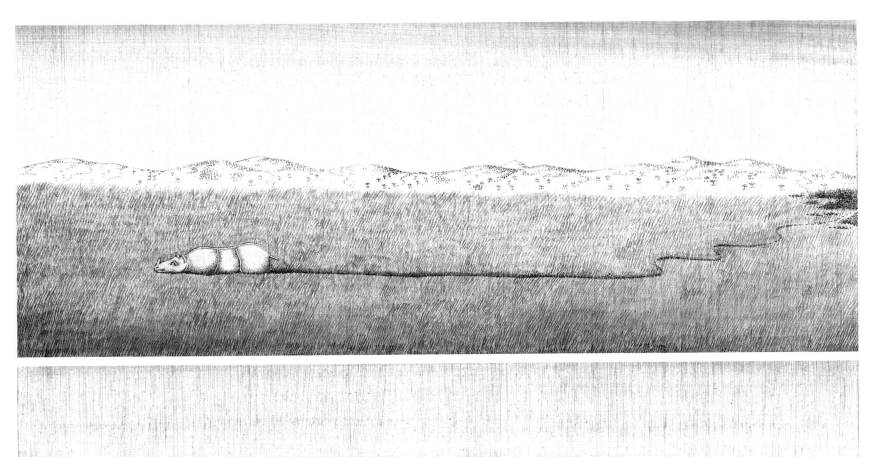

He sat down and thought about his friends,
the rainbow birds.
All of a sudden a humming filled the air.
Rhino looked up. The tree had come alive.

A shivering, buzzing swarm of wild bees hung over his head. Rhino ran and ran.

He came to the field of red poppies.
There, ready to pounce, was a hungry hyena.
Red bird cried, "This is no place for me!"
And he flew onto Rhino's back.

Rhino ran and ran and ran.
Soon they came to the banana grove.
There, ready to strike, was a big fat snake.
Yellow bird screeched, "This is no place for me!"
And he flew onto Rhino's back.

Rhino kept on running
and they came to the blue lake.
There, about to snap his great wide jaws,
was an enormous crocodile.
Blue bird shrieked, "This is no place for me!"
And he flew onto Rhino's back.

And Rhino kept right on running
until they were home
in the middle of the deep valley
somewhere behind the mountains.

And that is where they stayed.